The New BIRD in TOWN

Jamie L. B. Deenihan · Carrie Hartman

With the help of his forest estate agent,
Owl found the perfect home.

It had everything he needed . . .

. . . except new friends.

When no one called back, Owl swooped down to introduce himself.

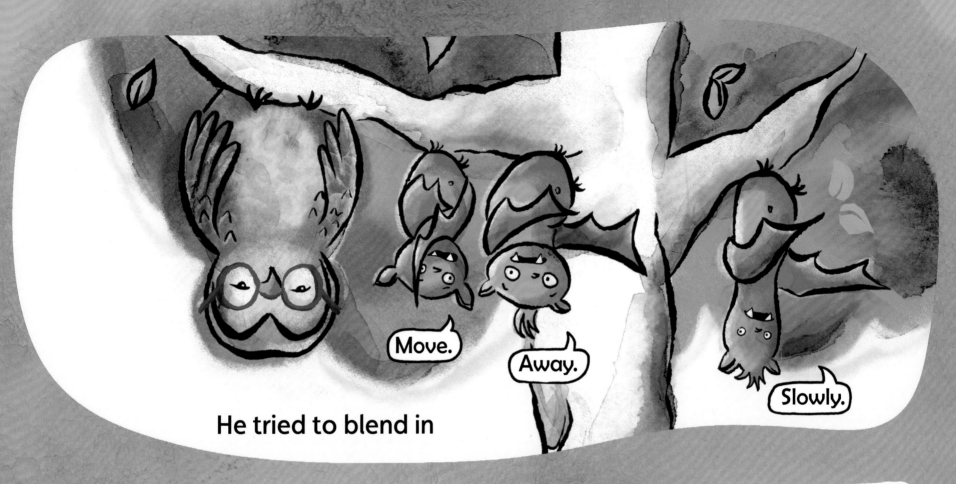

He tried to blend in

and offered to share his favorite food.   The new bird needed a new plan.

He made invitations,

decorated his tree,

and put on his favorite party outfit
and his friendliest face.

Welcome,
friends

Owl waited

and waited

and waited.

I'm sorry I scared you.

I'm sorry I panicked.

Your stripe makes you look tough.

I only spray when I'm in danger.

19

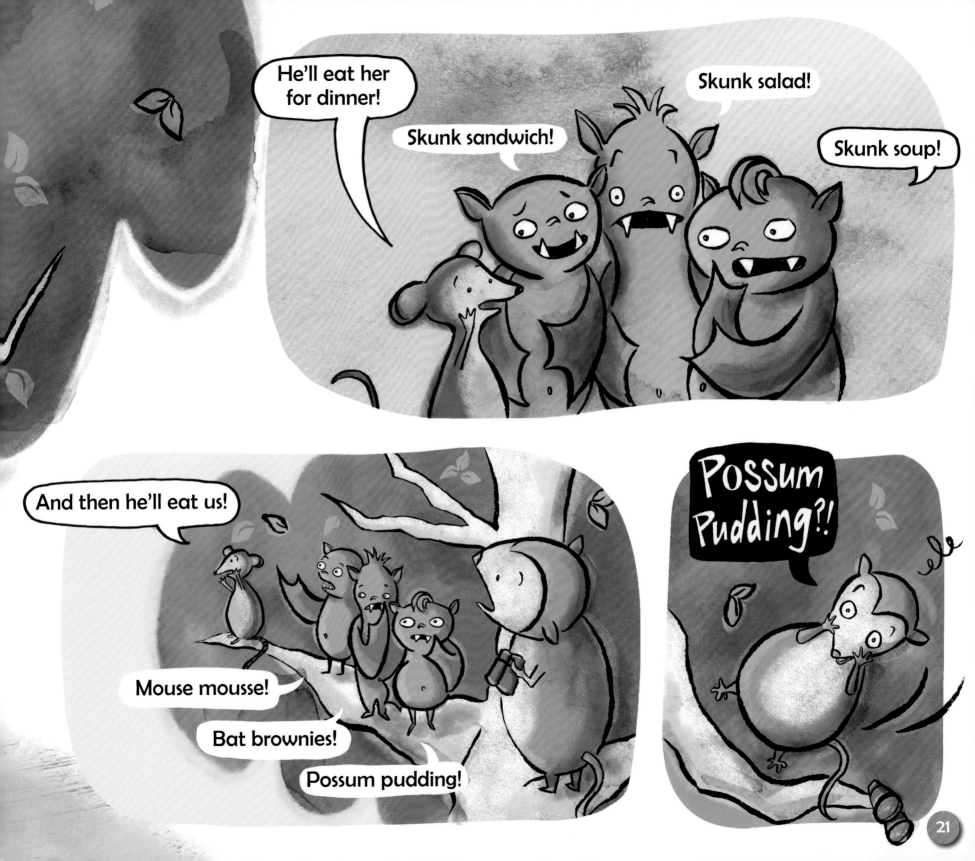

23

Owl's new friends walked him home.

All the excitement tired Owl out. The new bird needed a nap.
His friends tucked him in.

When Owl woke up, Skunk wasn't the only new friend waiting
to give him a proper welcome.

COOKED FOR YOU, THAT'S WHO!

Owl's new home was perfect.
It had everything he needed,
including new friends.